Nella

BOOK ONE
A BALLPARK WORKER

BY CANDACE TAYLOR JOHNSON

Nella A Ballpark Worker Book | By Candace Taylor Johnson

ISBN 978-0615599151

Editor: Mark Farrell markfarrell@topcopyediting.com
Cover Design: Mary Ivory (ivyivory27@yahoo.com)
Text Design: Stephanie Lewis (23exchange@gmail.com)
Layout Design: Kathryn Burton (kburton.design@gmail.com)
Communication: Mychal Taylor

Knack-Time Book Publishing: Candace Taylor Johnson
E-mail Candacetj@gmail.com
Twitter @KnackTime
Facebook: Candace Taylor Johnson Knack-Time Books

Registration Number TXu1 799-359
Printed in the United States Of America

To the vision team - Shelly Bethea, Christopher Pouncy, Gail Taylor, Clifford McGarity, Terrell Taylor, and Roderick Wisdom.

"A special thanks to everyone around the world who collects sports memorabilia which has become the most precious invaluable souvenirs in our lives. My deepest gratitude to Michael Johnson & family & friends for their encouragement. Special appreciation goes out to my fellow authors in the Shelby Township Writers Group."

- Candace Taylor Johnson

"Nella A Ballpark Worker is a drama fiction - exciting, alarming, stirring and impressively touching. I am a new author and will compose a Novella Italian meaning *new*. A composed dramactic fiction like the opera set to words. Knack-Time literature for your reading enjoyment. I assure you my readers Knack-Time books will lead you to read them more than once. This book is a situation literary fiction focusing on the happiness, and heartbreak of winning. A story which will require an open mind and a loose disposition. Think of this story as a roller coaster ride fast, exciting, and short. Welcome to the world of literary fiction! So sit back or stand with humor."

"Buckle your read-belt as you proceed to read, *NELLA A BALLPARK WORKER*."

Contents

Note to my readers

"Nella a ballpark worker is a Novella, a short novel meaning new fiction. Novella is from the Italian word Novella which means new. Characters, events, affairs, functions experiences, invents, and mechanics are just the active mind of the Novelist. Remember this book is to be looked at as a Novel."

"Sincerely, The Author"

CHAPTER I

Introduction

Wonderful! This is my first day of work. What will I wear?

How will I style my hair? Anyway, I hope I am not nervous. I have never felt comfortable around crowds, but this time it will be worth it. I will wear a simple white shirt and a pair of blue jeans, then put my hair in a ponytail--I need a rubber band. I found one! Thank God it's blue. Like me, this job is blue, but I'm happy to have it since it's the middle of the season and I can't believe I'm working at the ballpark. The big and beautiful blue park, hard by the freeway, swims in a sea of green--trees on the outside, grass on the inside. I will be working in the uniform department behind the bullpen. The department is made up of two big locker rooms; one clean, the other dirty. There is also clean and dirty laundry rooms, as well as a place to store clean linen. An elevator leads to the third-floor offices; the security office is behind the bullpen. I work a late afternoon schedule on my first day. Traffic is light on my way to the park, and I find a free parking spot within sight of the park: no parking meter, no fire hydrant, not a single parking sign. I'll be cleaning the player's uniforms.

I'm nervous but put on a brave face. I want to present myself as a serious, good worker. I want the advantages that having confidence and being a good worker bring. I walk to the boss's office. Mr. Don is the supervisor of the souvenir store, uniform supply, and design. He smiles. I don't know if I should smile, remember, serious and brave. "Hello Nella, ready on your first day?" asked Mr. Don. "Yes, thank you, sir," I reply. "The game is starting in two hours," He said. "First of all, your job is to take every single one of these uniforms, to each player present in the dugout. Here is the list, and I will do your first walk with you Nella. Usually, the players are in a good mood." Mr. Don and I hang the uniforms on a courier cart and roll them down the hall. "Then, Nella, I will show you the laundry," he said. "Most important, here is your key and a hat." So, we put the courier with the uniforms on it in the clean linen room then we lock the door and proceed down the hall. "Nella, I will show you the dirty laundry room," he said. When Mr. Don and I walked in the dirty laundry room, there were two others workers present. "Nella, I would like you to meet Troy and Arika." "Hello," I said, greetings to my new co-workers. "Troy and Arika wash uniforms, towels, also socks as well as dry-clean attire then load-hang the uniforms," Mr. Don said.

"After the game, you will wash and collect the uniforms and get everything ready for the next game. Usually, there will be a list of attire the players need. We will return shortly to the clean linen room. Do you have any questions Nella?"

"I don't have any questions, Mr. Don," I reply.

Next we go back to the office by the sign. We go in and sit down. "Nella, this is a list of rules; read the rules, and take some time, then sign on the bottom where the X is," said Mr. Don. "Most important, do not sign the list of rules if you have any questions. I will leave you and will be back soon." The rules read as follows:

1. All property of the organization uniforms, socks, towels, jackets, baseball hats, and souvenirs are to be kept in good condition and are not subject to personal use. Vandalism and careless actions will be audited and may be prosecuted by law.

2. All employees must look and act in a professional, civil manner.

3. Employees must not enter private entrances.

4. No fraternization is allowed between employees, employers, customers, or fans of either team.

5. An employee's first paycheck will be held for one week.

6. All employees must be ready at the time of shift, usually two hours before the game time.

7. Each employee must wear a baseball hat.

8. All keys must be returned to security at the end of each shift, and employees may not remove them from the site.

9. Special duties are to be performed with the consent of management.

10. All employees are to mandate.

Wait, let me think, breathe--I'm confused. Should I ask Mr. Don a question about the timing of the check? I need that pay in two weeks. The rest of my tuition to the design school is due to be paid in a couple of weeks, but I assume they will let me start because I'm a regular student and just need to wait a few more days after the deadline. By then I will have already have received my paycheck.

"Nella, it's an hour to game time," said Mr. Don. "Do you have any questions?" "No," I replied.

I sign my name at the X - Nella O'Neal. "Time to pass out the uniforms to the players stated, Mr. Don." Ready, for the organization?

"Nervous, Nella?" asked Mr. Don. "Yes sir, Mr. Don," I replied.

Meanwhile, doubts raced through my mind: Will I be successful? It's an important job, and I'm fortunate to have it. I walked toward the clean linen room near Mr. Don's office. "Got your key, Nella?" "Yes, right here in my pocket," I replied. I opened the door; it was time to take the uniforms to the players.

I'm fascinated by the uniforms; they are so unique. Crafted from fine material, the uniforms are a designer's dream. I feel important, like a connoisseur of fashion dressing the runway model before a fashion show. We walk the short distance to the locker room, through a corridor, as I try to calm my nerves. I'm frantic as we approach.

"Finally! Here it is, Nella - the clean locker room," Mr. Don said. "Remember to knock."

I knock. "Come in," someone says. As I look around the wonderful clean locker room, I notice the nicely dressed men waiting to put on their uniforms for game day. "Gentlemen, this is Nella," said Mr. Don. "Today is her first day; make her feel welcome." Remember in the future men; put your used uniform in the dirty locker room for a special attire request. Sometimes, Nella, they request extra shirts to wear under their uniforms; maybe different socks; but they pick their own shoes. In the meantime, everybody is the same, and they will wear regular uniforms." Turning to the players, Mr. Don announced, "Fellows understand, please cooperate until Nella can get used to the system."

Mr. Don introduced me to the players individually. "Let's get started Nella this is Mark, known as Mark K and his uniform is right here first, here's your uniform Mark." Mr. Don said.

"Thank you," replied Mark. "You're pretty and, it's nice to meet you Nella." I can't believe he said that I'm pretty. I'm sort of embarrassed, because I am feeling not so pretty, with a baseball hat on my head.

We move on to the next player, and he thanks me. "Thank you, and good luck, sir," I reply. We continue down the line, and each thanks me. Then two of the other players look at me and laugh; I ignore them. Two other men are professional and serious, so I must be serious as well. Then one of them says, "Hello, my name is Aaron, and this is Josh." They both say thank you, and finally I respond.

"You're welcome and good luck." I'm thinking the men are pretty nice, but I'm happy the introductions are over.

"Good job Nella," said Mr. Don.

"Thank you sir," I replied.

"I'll walk back with you to the dirty laundry room. Any questions or problems, don't hesitate to ask me."

The men seem nice, but above all I need to set a good example.

"I hope you can organize the attire they need. Of course, it will take a couple of days to learn how to do it. They also go on the road, so we prepare while they're not here. Next, you will work with Troy and Arika, and then relieve Arika from duty. Then, you and Troy will finish after the game, mostly in the clean laundry room. The uniforms need to be picked up from the dirty locker room. They will be in a big hamper on wheels. You wash them, hang them, and then take them to the clean linen room for the next day.

I'll replace damaged uniforms. Write their name down on paper if I am not here and, put it under my door. "

"Thank you, Mr. Don."

"Good luck, Nella."

"Where shall I start?" I asked Troy.

"Folding towels," said Troy. Troy is about 6 feet tall with a conservative look: clean-cut black hair and brown eyes. "Half-an-hour to game time, Arika," Troy said.

Troy has a small television on the dryer. Wow, what an advantage, I thought. There he is again on television; the one that said I was pretty. I'm thinking he is very good looking man, but silly for calling me pretty.

"Turn it up, Arika," Troy said.

"Okay Troy shut the door."

"Arika I hope they win!" exclaimed Troy. "That is nice they let you all watch the game," I said.

"But we turn it off if we get busy, you are working here now and, we do need the extra help. "Congratulations

Nella, you have a good job, he said. We thought they would

hire a man, but they hired a woman." "Troy, I'll start folding

the towels now, because I like to stay busy."

Time passed quickly, and they won all-right, good

job! I thought.

"Yes, yes, yes! Time's flying, so time for break," said

Arika.

"You going to break, Nella?"

"No, I will stay until it's time to get the dirty laundry

cart." I replied. "What time do they finish changing?"

"About an hour, so we take break," said Troy. "Okay,

"I will sit." I replied.

I was feeling kind of anxious. I hoped the players

had changed and were gone. Meanwhile, I had a soda and

relaxed. I was excited that the order of the day is going fine;

they won, therefore I like the job at this point. I'm trying not

to feel nervous on my first day, so I will try to trade being nervous for being patient, but I worry about my check almost three weeks! I hope I can make it.

They are finished, and we are back.

"Nella, you can go get the used uniforms in the hamper from the dirty locker room." Troy said. "Make sure you knock. If there is no answer, use your key."

"OK Troy, I'll return soon," I replied.

This place is so nice; the walls are very attractive. Moving along, I didn't notice that sign--it says "CLEAN LAUNDRY ROOM: DO NOT ENTER."

A little further down: "LOCKER ROOM." I knock no answer. Then I remember Troy said "use my key and go in." There is the hamper full of the beautiful uniforms, ready to be washed. The cart is heavy to push and I am responsible for it, but think maybe Troy should get this hamper; it is hard to roll.

"I'm back Troy, and here are the uniforms," I said.

"Put your gloves on and go through them," said Troy.

"Wait Nella use that magic spray for the tough stains."

"These giant washers are nice," I remark. "Only one kind of washing soap to use well, they are separated."

Troy replied, "Put them in the washer, Nella. Start it at about 20 minutes; the buzzer will sound when they are done."

Buzzer; finally, they are finished.

"Nella, now take your time and put them in the dryer," said Troy. "Let me help you."

We wait 30 minutes. The buzzer sounds again, and they are finished.

"Nella, you can find their name on the shirt, and printed inside the tag on the pants." Troy said, "These are the hangers, and they are ready to hang."

They turned out nice. Arika returned and said, "Time for me to go home. Have a good night you two."

"Arika, nice meeting you," I said.

"Same to you, Nella," Arika said. Meanwhile, I admire the uniforms as I hang them. I feel they are my special project; finally, I'm done.

"Nella, Mr. Don suggests I close with you," said Troy. "Don't forget to take your keys to security."

The uniform rack on wheels is lightweight now, and I'll push it to the clean linen room and lock it.

Goodbye, Nella," Troy said. "Time for us to go."

"Nice meeting you, Troy," I replied. Wait! Troy. What will I do with the baseball hat?

"Leave the hat with security and get it later," replied Troy. "When you come back, I'm sure they'll let you keep it."

The day went well; I stayed busy. It's time to go home. I approach my car. This is the perfect place to park I think. hopefully, the same spot will be available tomorrow.

Sometimes my car won't start; I have to get another soon. I drive home thinking of the check that will arrive so I can enjoy my favorite foods. Today, I excercised patience. I'm feeling starved, so I'll eat an apple, potato chips, and drink some water. Then I will take a shower and sleep.

CHAPTER II

Nella's Independent Day

Upon my arrival for my second day at the ballpark, the same parking spot is available. "Hello, Mr.

Don," I say upon entering the park.

"Hello Nella; did you have a good evening? Did Troy help you? "Get your key from security first said, Mr. Don."

I don't want to hear this because, all I can think about is that I'm having a bad hair day, and want to cover it up.

"No, let me go right now," I replied. "Mr. Don, what about the baseball hat is the hat my own, and can I take it home?" I asked.

"Yes, Nella," Mr. Don replied."

I thought, Nella a ballpark worker, don't doubt yourself. What a relief, I think. I'll go to security for the keys, and hat then return to the office.

"You're on your own," said Mr. Don. "Just one thing: This is a list of attire. If the players have any suggestions, check the item and write their name next to it. If they have any special requests, I need to know."

"Yes sir," I replied.

"Good luck, Nella, the ball game starts in two hours."

I have butterflies in my stomach; I breathe and will not smile, because it seems unprofessional. I approach the locker room and knock. "Come in." It's Mark. "Hello, and thank you," he said.

"Does anyone have any special attire requests?" I asked each team member while passing out their uniforms. "Thank you, gentlemen, I must proceed to the clean laundry room."

The dirty laundry room is down the corridor, not too far from the clean laundry room.

"Hello Troy. Where is Arika?" I asked.

"She doesn't work today, he replied."

The day is almost over. They lost, and the atmosphere is quiet. "I have everybody's uniform but Mark's, Troy," I said.

"Nella, he is probably practicing again," Troy replied. "You can expect him to practice sometimes after the game. "Come on, I will show you: See? There he is."

"Where?"

"Right through there."

"Oh I see him in the ballpark," I said. "Thanks Troy."

"Nella tomorrow it'll be different; they'll be on the road. Look, you're not working; you have the day off. I'm going Nella. You'll do a good job. If you need anything, ask security."

"Wait, Troy, I don't have Mark's uniform. Here he comes now," Troy said.

"Next time, don't wait. He knows where to put it, or he can get another one.

"Hello! Sorry," Mark says as he approaches.

"Thanks just leave it on the table." Do you need help finishing or taking the cart down to the clean linen room?" he asked.

"No Mark, you can't come in here." I said.

He replied, "Why not? I used to help James, the guy that worked here before you," Mark said. "See, I can hang."

"No, wait, don't!"

"Please look, I helped James."

I'm thinking, that isn't the correct way to do it.

"Excuse me," I said.

"Well, we lost," Mark said.

"Sorry, I have work to finish," I said.

"I was just trying to say, that's why I'm late with the suit. Why don't you smile?" asked Mark.

"The position doesn't require me to smile, express happiness, or speak to you or anybody else." I said. "What do you mean?" They have rules Mark.

"You have that look of: not amused."

"I'm working trying to achieve this task. Don't you read the sign? Do not enter. Mark, you shouldn't be in here."

"That's ridiculous," he says. "You wash, dry, and deliver the uniforms!"

I said, "Mark, with all due respect, you don't know anything about me."

He said, "I'm sure your job is laborious, but you should work on that temper. Nella, remember I offered to help you."

Then he left, I thought he's ridiculous. They lost. The morning has arrived and this is a day off from working at the ballpark. I'll sit on the porch and read or draw apparel, or write in my journal.

Dear Journal,

I have been at this job for a couple of days now and today I'm off. Yesterday I practiced patience there and making sure I organized the laundry correctly. They lost, but, there was still a job to be done. The neighbors are currently having another disagreement. I love to draw and design clothes and will make them when I get another sewing machine. Quiet. Stop! That's the neighbor--they argue; it makes me sad because I can hear them disagree about who is using

29

the car. Fuss when they arrive home. My opinion is he's controlling. I recall the day when she cried. The car remained after she asked him if she could drive it. Fearless, I requested to take her where she wanted to go. "No!" he said, "Stay out of our business." I embraced her that day and went to my bedroom and shut the door, feeling empathy and tears that matched. Thank God I work tomorrow morning.

THE END

CHAPTER III

Winning Day

"Good morning Nella, said Arika." The men are

still on the road so today we can catch up. I'll show you how

to prepare uniforms, attire, and accessories properly since

they are gone."

"It's so quiet around here," I said.

"They'll be back tomorrow and the noise will return

Arika said." After a few days of work, I can say I really like

the job and enjoy it here." What a great morning. I got off

early and arrived home safely, and will enjoy the rest of my day resting before the big day tomorrow.

The next day, my car failed to start, so I asked the neighbors for a jump. "Excuse me. Can you help me? My car won't start; I need a jump," I said.

"Yes," they said. I just don't see why they argue. "Try it," the neighbor said.

The car started--good. "Thank you I said." I made it on time. The men are back; it's a-regular day, time to pass out uniforms. Today, I don't have to knock. The door is open to the clean locker room. "Hello men! Mark, here is your uniform," I said.

"Thank you," he said with a smirk. The two guys next to him are always laughing. Aaron--he seems to be nice; comfortable, but serious. Then there is that man Josh--I think he is relaxed but concerned. "I cannot wait to leave this team as a free man," said Aaron. "Yes," said Josh. I'm thinking that is why they are laughing--he's leaving.

"Troy, can I ask you a question? I was wondering the other day Mark was trying to help. Is he allowed?"

"Mark knows he's not allowed to," Troy responded while watching the game on television. "He used to help the other guy who worked here, James."

"Why did he leave?" I asked.

"He just didn't come back," said Troy. "I guess he found something else."

"That man Aaron--is he leaving?"

"Yes, he is going to--another team."

"That's what he said, he is so sarcastic."

"He can be. He is the better player," said Troy.

I thought Mark was.

The score is tied 3 to 3. A victory for Mark! Mark made the home winning run in the 9th inning. The men there they go. They are so loud. "WE won - celebration time! GO! WE WON! GO, GOOD JOB! TIME TO CELEBRATE WINNING," the players shouted.

"I have to go Nella; have a good night," Troy said.

I'm thinking Mark might come in here again; I would rather he didn't--I get nervous. I can get in trouble. I need my job. Well, he didn't this time. So, it's time to take the keys to security. A good time to go home, such a nice night! When they win, a spirit of happiness fills the air. I hope my car will start, but it doesn't. What will I do now? Take the bus, or ask for a jump for my car? Out of despair, I ask another person whose car is parked nearby. "Excuse me, sir, can I have a jump?" He tries, but it doesn't work. The car won't start. What else can go wrong? I have to catch the bus or sit here; I look in my purse but I have no money for a cab.

At that moment, a car pulled up to mine. The dark-tinted window rolled down--it was Mark. "Mark, is that you?"

"Of course, Nella," he said.

"You shouldn't be out here, Mark."

"Nobody is out here," he replied. "This is your car--is it running. Why are you out here?"

"I'm just waiting for a friend."

"It won't start, will it? Let me try." Again, he is trying to help me. Let me take a moment and breathe.

"No thank you, I said."

"Move over, let me try."

I am embarrassed.

"Do you need a ride, Nella?"

"No thank you, Mark."

"Nella, you're part of our team now--you think I'm going to leave you out here? That would be the wrong thing to do."

"Well, I guess, except I live in the North End. What about the big celebration?"

"That's later," he laughed.

"This is a nice car, Mark."

"Hello," said the car.

"What is your address Nella?"

"Hello," the car said again.

"Now tell the car your address," said Mark.

"555 North Street, right off the freeway. Your car can talk! That is amazing."

"The car responding. "SEAT BELTS PLEASE, ENJOY YOUR RIDE, 15 MINUTES TO DESIGNATION, AT MAXIMUM SPEED. PLEASE MANEUVER. ENTER THE FREEWAY GOING UP."

"Please don't go too fast, Mark!"

"The car can tell you if highway patrol is one mile ahead or a mile back," he replied. Then the car said, "YOU HAVE REACHED YOUR DESIGNATION; PLEASE ENJOY THE REST OF YOUR DAY."

"We're here. This is your place, Nella?" Mark asked.

"Yes, I live downstairs not the best but it's a roof over my head. Mark, your car is very impressive. Thanks! Just, don't tell anybody, and have fun celebrating."

"What about your car?"

"I'll pick it up later or tomorrow."

"Why don't you let my man fix the car and have it back in the morning?"

"No, Mark."

"Well you look confused, Nella."

"Fine, that will be good," I replied.

"Thanks, no problem. Hold on, I need the key. Nella, you're doing a good job."

"Thanks, Mark, be careful around here. It's good that you have tinted windows."

Next, "Hum, hum, hum let me check my mailbox." Why is Mark still parked there? He's on the phone.

"Hello, my man." My man is Mark's partner who helps him with business and decisions. "There's a car at the ballpark. I think it's a gray older model. It needs a starter. Can you tow it and fix it? I'll bring the key to the celebration, are you going to be there?"

"Yes, I'll be there, Mark, and I'll have the car fixed."

"Thank you my man."

"No problem, Mark. Good job on the winning run."

Checking my mail--What is this? A post card; they canceled my date to start school? I ask you, what else can go wrong? As I walk up the stairs, I feel I have nothing.

My future is in doubt; I would like to move and then buy another car, but I need to finish design fashion school. No dreams. The tears will not stop, so to bed I go. While I lay here I can't rest, so I write in my journal.

Dear Journal,

I just got off work. Not the best day. My car wouldn't start and it was embarrassing. One of the players gave me a ride home, and they cancelled my course at school.

THE END

I'll call my classmate, Cenita. "Hello, Cenita. I'm in shock they cancelled my course."

"Nella, I can't believe she didn't give you time to pay your tuition," Cenita said. "Maybe you should have called."

"I thought I could attend, since I'm part of the program. Not only that but I thought I would get my paycheck."

"Nella, it's been two weeks."

"They hold the check back."

"That's odd. Well, I will keep you in my prayers."

"Thanks, Cenita."

"Goodbye, Nella."

CHAPTER IV

Heart of Celebration

Celebration! "I'm here, Mark."

Mark is daydreaming about a heart and Nella.

"My man welcome; here is the key to the car."

"Don't worry about it, Mark. Whose car is that anyway?"

"A worker at the ballpark; I need another favor."

"Here come the girls, Mark."

"Hi, Mark, are you off tomorrow? Want to stay up dancing, drinking?"

"No thanks, but how about drinks for you girls?" he asked.

"Thanks Mark!"

From across the room, Mark shouted, "I scored the winning run in the 9th, Aaron. Tonight is your turn to pay for the drinks!"

"I'll only pay for the beer, Mark," said Aaron.

"My man Aaron is so cheap," Mark said. "That's why I'm better than him."

Aaron and Josh both stare at Mark on the other side of the bar. "Aaron look at Mark--he thinks he can get all the girls, maybe even Nella. What do you think Aaron?" asked Josh.

"Josh, I don't think so," replied Aaron.

The two of them discuss their conversation. The bartender is waiting for them to order.

"You want to play a game? Game!" Aaron said, "Josh, a million dollar wager on Nella." Think it will be worth that much Aaron?"

"I don't know, some women only choose to have a child when they are married," Aaron replied.

"One year Aaron," said Josh. "Look at Mark. He is too arrogant, conceited, and stubborn. Mark needs to grow up."

The bartender waits patiently for a request. "What would you gentlemen like to drink?" he asks.

"I will have a regular beer, and so will Josh," said Aaron. "No non-alcoholic beer for us tonight."

"Aaron paying for the ladies," the bartender said.

"I'll pay for the girls; no problem," said Aaron.

The bartender returns with the drinks for everybody.

The team chants, "Cheers!"

Mark sits, thinking about my big red heart: "I'll give Nella a gift of money, because I feel terrible about her car and where she lives. I believe she deserves better. Most important, I'll need an envelope that can warm her heart."

"My man, I need another favor," he said. "Can you have a very unique envelope printed? I will pick it up tomorrow night when we play poker. Then I'll pay you for the envelope and fixing the car."

Another day, and looks like my car is fixed. They dropped it off this morning with the key, which was in the mailbox. Cenita said she would pray for me. So I will have faith. Tomorrow, I'll thank Mark for having my car repaired. Finally, the day is here. They have an early game, and I have an early day at work. I can't wait to get my check. I've worked so hard since, I first started this job.

"Hello, men, I'm here with the uniforms. Mark, here you are."

"Then I said, next, gentleman, and so on." Finished in the meantime, I can't wait until the day is over. I'm disappointed, and don't feel much like smiling. So I return to the clean laundry room to work. Someone is knocking. Yes, who is it?" I asked.

"Mark K, Nella--can I talk to you for a minute? How is your car working?"

"Good I replied, thank you so much, Mark. I just want to go home."

"Nella, I'm wishing you felt better," Mark said. "There are times when life seems hard, but eventually it gets better. Nella, I worked so hard practicing, taking care of myself physically and emotionally. We didn't have much growing up, but I focused on making it to first, second, and third finally to owning my own home. The harder you work and stay in good spirit the more confident you become."

"Nella, stay in good spirit."

"Thanks, Mark I'm just tired."

"Nella, you should be excited. Today is an early day. Then he said, Nella, I know I'm excited. Look, Nella I have something for you."

"What is that? Is it an envelope or a card? That's so cute. Who drew that?"

"This is for you, I sense you need help," said Mark.

"Mark, wait, stop for a minute."

"Nella, everybody should have what they need here. I have what I need, and want to help you." No Mark.

"Hold on Mark! I can't take this."

"Remember Nella, you are part of the team like all of us."

Well, I thought, should I take it? The envelope is very attractive, and maybe it might help. I put it in my purse.

"Mark, please do not tell anybody you gave me this."

"Smile and have a good day, Nella."

I walked back to the laundry room. "Troy, can I ask you something? Is Mark really nice?" Yes, Nella, he has helped so many people." Arika said. "Mark is about the best and will give you the shirt off his back. On occasion, he has lunch, dinner, whatever we like delivered to us here at the ballpark."

Troy said. "Especially the delicious pizza topped with everything from the pizzeria."

I thought: "Keep this to myself about the envelope." Thank God, the work day is finally over.

I go quickly to my car. When I get in my car I'm so anxious to open this envelope. I look around and hope nobody can see me. Then I open it.

This man Mark has given me $5,000 in cash. I can't believe it, so I need to breathe first. Should I take this money or give it back? I decided to keep the $5,000.

The first thing to do is fill up my money card. The next stop will be to the beauty shop to get a makeover. I arrive at my favorite salon to have my hair washed, conditioned, and styled. My hair is natural curly; I just want it to be beautiful and manageable. I like to be natural, no makeup for my face, but as for my nails a manicure, and my feet a pedicure. I love to shop. I'll purchase dresses, then a couple pair of blue jean pants, and blouses. Finally, I'll buy a couple pairs of shoes. On my way now to the market to buy: milk, bread, wine, fish and cheese. I feel happiness loading my car like I'm celebrating! So, time to go to the Pizzeria, and order takeout pizza. I can't wait to get home to pay my tuition for design school. I think I'll sit at the computer, pay for design school, and eat my Pizza topped with everything. I feel really good, but I hope it's for the right reason. Well, Mark was right when he said I must stay in good spirit, so I finished eating, turned on the music, and celebrated while trying on the new clothes! These dresses are so beautiful.

Then, I hear a loud voice. "Where have you been?" Sounds to me like the neighbors, drama! I turn the music down. "Leave me alone, she cried. If I told you where I was you probably won't believe me; besides all you do is drink and sleep."

"He said, shut up!" Unexpectedly, I hear her cry. I hope that she is going to be all-right this time. It's so sad. Tomorrow I'll look for a place close to the ballpark.

The guys are on the road. Regardless, this morning I will report to work. Mr. Don would like to train me in the souvenir store. Not only will I wash, and sell the products, I'll order, design, and buy them. This is good news. The tour of the store is pleasant. I'm learning the important job of inventory and make buying decisions that we'll eventually learn in school. "Nella, this is a big step--you'll start the day after tomorrow," said Mr. Don. "We're finished here."

"Thank you, Mr. Don," I replied.

"Have a good day, Nella," he said.

I have to go to school and I am excited; I also made it on time, thank God. "Today, we are learning about developing originality to be the best, and the assignment is to design a garment." The garment must be original of course socks are my favorite to design. I have a great idea--I'll design an original shirt for Mark. After school I usually go home and work on my project. That is what I will do this evening. But first I'll stop at the apartments near the ballpark to see if any are available for rent. Good news--there is one available, so I pay the deposit and plan to move at the end of the week. One more stop to make--to the store. I will buy new furniture and a new sewing machine and quality material. I can't believe I got a start on my finances with the money Mark gave me. I've arrived home excited and can't wait to work on my original design.

First, I need to imagine how Mark feels. Mark seems to be happy. He likes to see people do generous deeds, as well as do them himself. He performs acts of kindness, and he has a good spirit. "I will call the shirt, Spirit." The shirt will be a t-shirt with embroidery on the collar. After I drew the shirt, I loved how it looks. However, I decide to design Mark's shirt with, different embroidery on the collar and at the bottom. The customers will only have the embroidery on the collar. The two garments will include his name on a small but, prominent place on the tag. When I go back to work, I will get permission from Mr. Don to sell it in the store.

"Mr. Don, I'd like to show you a shirt I designed for Mark." Mr. Don thought it was appealing. "Nella, I love the shirt! Show it to Mark immediately, and ask him what prices we should charge for adults and children."

The day becomes better. "Nella, I have your check," Mr. Don said.

"Thank you," I said. I thought I almost forgot about the check. Most importantly, I must put it away to pay Mark back, because he helped me get started.

I'm so excited to find Mark and show him the shirt. Usually, I forbid him to come in here because of the "Do Not Enter" sign. There he is.

"Mark, can I talk to you?" I ask. "It will just take a minute. Come in and shut the door. Surprise! I designed this shirt. This is the original one made for you, and this shirt is for adults, and the one for children is slightly different.

"Nella I love it!" Mark said.

"What do you think of the price--$25 for adults and, $15 for children?" I asked.

"I agree with the price, Nella," Mark said.

"Thank you, Mark," I said. "Good luck with the game and enjoy the shirt--it belongs to you."

Mark suddenly kissed me on the cheek. I smiled, and then he tried to kiss me in the mouth. Feeling of doubts lead me to keep it closed. I will not open my mouth, but I couldn't breathe. So I opened it for air. Then he did. "I really do love the shirt Nella. I would like to see you later this weekend. Can I have your number? "Well you can't have my number and my address has changed I don't know Mark. "My new address. I'll think about giving it to you later."

"Glad to see you smile. Thanks for the shirt," he said. Then he left.

Why don't I feel excited? Telling Mark, I might give him my address? Unseemly, unprofessional; it changed my mood. I hope he is not trying to pursue me. I was just doing my job, designing the shirt. I don't feel comfortable with him in here, except just this time to show him the shirt. I will think about giving him my address at the end of the week. I hope he doesn't ask me again, this week is going very well after all I finally received my paycheck; I have a new t-shirt I've designed for my class, which will help me both at school and at work; and what's more, I really like the job, except that Mark kissed me.

CHAPTER V

Excitement

Later that week, I gave him my address. This weekend, they are on the road and he is visiting the night he gets back. I'm off this weekend, and nervous during the time I moved into my new apartment. I didn't have much to move. The things I shopped for worked fine. What a weekend I'm feeling excited about Mark coming to visit tomorrow, at the same time sensitive. I bought some great wine and non-alcoholic beer, as well as fruit, cheese, and fresh bread.

Finally, the day is here. I wore a dress I bought and styled my hair hanging down. Meanwhile, I have mixed feelings about whether this is the right thing to do.

My job at this point is so important. I will tell Mark how I feel. The doorbell rings. There he is.

"Just a minute, welcome, Mark," I said.

"Nella, you look prettier, different than at the job," said Mark.

"Would you like some beer or wine, Mark?" I ask. "A toast to the shirt I designed for you? How was the road trip?"

"Good, thank you. I thought about you the whole time, Nella," said Mark.

"I thought about you too, Mark. I am not sure about how we are getting along like this." "I like you," he said.

"Why do you like me, Mark?"

"You excite me, Nella."

"Mark, I excite you at the job? That's silly. We have to stay focused on our jobs," I replied.

"Right now, I am focused on you, Nella."

"Well, I am trying to focus on my job. I work in the store, and I like the men also the customers; soon I'll be designing for the other men. I love to take care of the uniforms, Mark. I like the job I don't want to go anywhere," I said.

"Sure it is not too much for you?" he asked. "Don't work too hard. I like your place it is really close to the ballpark."

"Thanks, and here's your drink, Mark."

"A toast to the shirt. Great job, Nella, but can I start where we left off?" Mark asked.

He kissed me again, then picked me up, carried me to the room, laid me on the bed, and started to take my dress off. My drink!

"What about the job, Mark?"

"Forget about the job, Nella."

It is happening. He is now kissing me all over my body. "See I get excited every-time I look and think about you Nella, laying here next to you," said Mark. "You're lovely."

It happened. We made love. Then both of us fell asleep. Later that night, I awoke to Mark next to me. "Mark you have to go."

"I want to stay; I'm definitely calm and relaxed," he said. He turned over, next grabbed my arm, and pulled me to the other side of the bed, it's happening again.

"Nella, you feel so good."

"Please Mark, you have to leave," I said. Finally, I got out of bed, took a shower, and got ready to go to school.

"Mark, will you get up soon? I have to make my bed!

"No Nella, can I get some sleep?" he said. "Last night, I just got off a plane. I'll make the bed."

"Mark, you have to leave soon, okay? I said. "Mark? Did you hear me? MARK?"

I am not surprised. He is back asleep. I can only imagine. He is exhausted and needs the rest after a long weekend on the road.

I am back at school and very excited to show the class my assignment. I presented my design to the class. The original shirt I designed for Mark, as well as the one for the customers that's slightly different. Then I shared with the class how excited I am to design original shirts for other players. Class went well today. On my drive home, I thought about what Mark did to me last night. The love we made over and finished. It was amazing. I arrive home. Mark's car is still here. Even though I'm in wonder, I will not do it anymore. I told him to leave.

"Mark, I can't believe you're still here," I said. I can get in trouble for this! They have a strict rule: No fraternization with the players. I don't want it to be a problem at the job. It was one wonderful night, Mark."

"What about me, Nella?" he asked. "How do you think I feel? This is real for me, and this is my business." I laughed. "That's not funny."

"I said. "Well, I want to keep my position, and I hope nobody at the job finds out."

"Nella, they will see it in your eyes," he said.

"Thanks for an awesome night."

Then Mark asked for a hug?

"Just a hug," I said.

I'm thinking, "Great, a hug. That is how it should have been when I showed him the shirt, a hug instead of a kiss."

"Goodbye, Mark," I said.

Then he left. When I went to my room, I saw that he did make the bed.

Back at work; I feel frightened that Mark is telling people what happened. If he does, I know he could never be loyal.

"Hi Troy," I said.

"Nella, Mr. Don will like to see you," he said.

Suddenly, I feel nervous my eyes. I wonder. What if he knows? Yes, I will go now.

"You want to see me, Mr. Don?" I ask.

"Yes, shut the door, Nella," he said. The shirt sold out! Congratulations! Plus, twenty more ordered. I want to get your permission to have more shirts made."

"You have my permission," I said.

"I will clarify it with Mark tonight," Mr. Don said. "Take it easy, present the uniforms, and then close the store."

"Thank you, Mr. Don," I said.

That was a close call--I thought he was going to inquire about Mark. Now it is time to go down to the men. The door is open. Of course, I am nervous after yesterday, but because of the success of the shirt I am brimming with confidence.

Mark is looking at me and, smiling. I turned and looked at Aaron and Josh, they're staring at me and Mark. They don't look happy. I heard Josh say, "Aaron, look."

"Here is your uniform, and t-shirt Mark," I said.

Finally, I finished distributing all of the uniforms, and everybody said thank you, including Aaron and Josh. I feel a little at ease, but not confident.

Later, while working in the store, I hear someone say "Mark, get the baseball!" He missed, and they're not winning! "Safe!" The Umpire shouted! Then someone else said, "Oh, come on Mark!"

I can imagine them in the dugout, Aaron, Josh and, the others saying they think me and Mark is going out especially with the look on their faces in the locker room.

"Arika, turn the television down, here comes Mark," Troy said. "Listen, Mark is kicking the lockers and you can hear him say, 'DAMN! I can't believe this. DAMN! DAMN!"

He's angry, and is not winning the game. Meanwhile Mr. Don has told me the manager wants to see me. At that moment, I knew I'd be in trouble.

"Nella, give me five minutes and I'll go with you," Mr. Don said. "Thanks for waiting." I asked? What does he want, Mr. Don? "I don't know," Mr. Don stated. "You shouldn't worry; you're doing a great job. Sir you asked to see me? "Yes, Nella sit down. Nella, we have a strict rule here that states-no fraternization with the players. Today we overheard the players talking, and your name was the topic. I'm just warning you; watch out for them. Especially Aaron and Josh, eventually Aaron is leaving. Trust me if they want to find you; they will find you. It's just not wise Nella, said the manager. Any problems, report it to me as well as Mr. Don, and we'll make sure everything is done by the rules. Troy, will take the uniforms to the players, and you can finish the clean laundry." I replied. "Yes sir thanks for your concern." "You can go back Nella", said Mr. Don.

My heart is pounding. I thought they were going to ask about Mark? I guess Mark doesn't discuss his affairs, but as for me it stops now. Time to focus on the position, so I'll discuss with Mark that I'm only here to work; organizing the uniforms then go home. Today is good news; and bad news. The good news is the shirt I designed for Mark has sold out on the other hand they lost. I have good news for them. They can expect me to be a worker at the ballpark. Marks uniform isn't here. He must be late again.

"Looking for this? Yes, Mark. The shirt sold out Nella! Want to celebrate? Mark, I can't; our relationship means business; no pleasure especially here at the ballpark. What are you talking about? Today I received a lecture from the manager, and I think he knows." Mark replied, "I don't tell my business, and I'm not here to make them happy concerning my affairs. Well he said I was the talk of the men during the game."

"Look, Mark maybe in the off season we can hang out, but not now, and you shouldn't be hanging here; in the linen room. I love my job even if it's; washing dirty laundry. I want to be successful."

"Nella, this job isn't everything," he replied.

"Well, you do your job winning, Mark, and I'll worry about my position organizing the uniforms. Mark, I want to start again the right way, and your money--I'll pay you back." I designed the shirt as a souvenir, and a contribution; to you Mark."

"I don't want the money back! Mark said, angrily."

"Quiet, somebody might hear you!"

"I don't want the money back. I gave the money to you, Nella."

"Mark, please let me do my job. Anyway, I'm a plain girl striving for success. Honestly, what do you want from me?"

"Nella, be yourself."

"I'm trying to be myself! Nella, a ballpark worker who works in the laundry, so let me do my job then go home. Holding Marks uniform in my hand, I said, "Mark please leave because, I have a lot of work to do!"

"Mark, sorry I screamed", but when I turned around he was gone. As I held his uniform in my hand, I felt terrible. On my way home I thought, he really wanted to be with me, but I put the job first. When I arrived home and lay down on my bed, we made love in. I could smell his cologne on my sheets. I feel tenderness, and thought oh Mark. Mark! This happened so fast. I am confused, because I overreacted, and disappointed him. The shirt sold out.

He was so excited about the shirt. With a rainbow of feelings, I wonder if there is still laughter, and love somewhere at the ballpark. Sobbing, I'll change my sheets and try to forget about Mark. This was not a good day after all. Tomorrow is a new day, and I'll practice on having a winning spirit.

CHAPTER VI

Stir of Emotions

With mixed feelings, I have to return to work at the ballpark. So I'll walk today, and try to remain in a good spirit, but feel a stir of emotions. I will work with Arika in the laundry. Troy is taking my place.

Troy knocked on the locker room door. "Here is your suit, Mark," Troy said. "Where's my t-shirt Troy, and where's Nella?" Mark asked.

"She has a different assignment," Troy said.

Mark considered Nella as exaggerating, the situation and having an attitude.

"I'll get your t-shirt later," Troy said. "Next man, next."

"Wait a minute, Troy this is not right--next, what is this? Where is Mr. Don? How can we win games like this?" Josh said.

Troy thinks it's funny, "he is hilarious!" Laughter filled the locker room! The men all laughed except for Mark. He sat for a moment and thought that Nella is trying to prove something.

"Nella, how can you deal with those men? All they do is complain, Troy said. Well, after that, I need a seat. Watching the game, Nella?"

"No," I replied.

"I'll go in the back to fold the towels, because I feel like an emotional roller coaster. I miss the men and feel bad that Mark and I had that disagreement." As I fold towels, Troy said, "Nella, don't worry about it. Mark should follow the rules. You don't see us hanging in the dugout or trying to manage the team. Mostly losing our composure like Mark, kicking the lockers and throwing things when he should concentrate on winning the game."

When I went in the back to fold towels, I thought that considering the short time I've been working here at the ballpark, I wanted to be professional, and make no mistakes. I thought manage. I made a big mistake, being with Mark. That's why they have rules. Good, the day is almost over and it-is time to get the soiled uniforms from the dirty locker room. Whose uniform is this on the floor? When I pick it up, I see that unfortunately, it's Mark's. I wonder if he did this on purpose. Look at this list. They need everything. I can see that this job can get difficult. Especially because Troy took my place, but I will see to it that the men have what they need. I need to take care of the uniforms, but fear that they might find out about me, and Mark. I know I'll be overcome with shame because he gave me that money, and being with him. I wonder if he will tell anybody.

Thank God the season is ending soon, so if they do find out about me taking that money from Mark, and the affair depending on where I work in the winter I'll come back and maybe they will forget. Mark said, He didn't tell anyone about his business.

Finally, I'm finished and feel my emotions stirring, and physically tired. I'm going home to sleep until it is time for work. They have an early game tomorrow. As I leave the ballpark, I am glad to be out of there walking, back to my apartment fine, thanks to Mark. I wonder if Mark is serious about the two of us. On this night, I can't sleep and lay in bed with anxiety about tomorrow morning at work, as well as school. Thinking about Mark, I know just the thing to do: apologize. In the meantime, I will get some sleep and imagine everything is going be okay.

Time to rise and go to work, but the most important thing today is to find Mark and talk to him. There he is practicing early today; I will wait until after the game. They lost, and it is quiet around here today. Well, looking for Mark. There he is, out there in the ballpark practicing. I just want to talk and tell him how very sorry I am, and here he comes. Let me get back to the linen room. So I go back in the linen room and turn around, pretending to be busy. From outside the room, I hear Mark's voice. "I can't believe we didn't score in the 7th, 8th, or 9th innings! Let me drop this off with the laundry lady. Time to celebrate losing!" Who is he talking to? He was talking to a girl! I didn't see her, but I heard her and him walk by laughing. Then he dropped his suit on the floor. The nerve of him, he should be ashamed. I am angry, humiliated and imagine screaming, THAT'S WHY YOU LOST!

He is going to make my job here at the ballpark difficult. I can't believe he did that. Should I tell Mr. Don?

No, I won't tell. I must be brave again. Well this afternoon, I'm going to school with anxiety. Breathe! He started with me; I can't imagine us holding hands, kissing with everybody watching. Or can it really happen?

I thought, Breathe again, Nella, you are just a ballpark worker because when I got to school, I was very upset, thinking about Mark, and how angry I was with him feeling his attitude has changed, and is now dirtier than my job. Sitting here, I feel a stir of emotions. I didn't even start on my new project, which is another original design. So I have to focus, and work on ignoring him, which is the best solution. Anyway, Troy said the season is almost over, and I must practice patience, and bravery the next time at work. "It doesn't matter anyway, the day after tomorrow I'll look for another job," I think.

Back to work now. As I walk to the ballpark, I'm thinking me, Nella a ballpark worker, and have hope that it will be a good day. The day actually goes well. I worked in the store and then collected uniforms from the dirty locker room. Mark's uniform is on the floor again--anguish! Another stir of emotions, I feel humiliated.

"Not again!" Should I quit my job? Suddenly, I'm having an emotional breakdown, so I turn around and cry, hoping nobody sees or hears me. Knock, knock! As I turned around, I see it was Aaron, and he asked to come in.

"I left some, Nella. Are you alright?"

"No, Aaron, I mean I'll live."

"What's wrong, Nella? Wait, before you answer that, I see Mark left his uniform on the floor again. He's a rude dude--I'll pick it up!"

"No, Aaron it's my job!"

"No it's not, Nella, I got it--see? If he keeps doing this, you'll need a raise and I'll need a bonus," he said, laughing! "Are you alright now?"

"Yes thank you Aaron."

"Nella, don't let Mark break you. Just ignore him and leave it the next time. Let him get a new one and he'll see that the new one won't fit."

Now I'm laughing. "Aaron, that's funny!"

"I have to go, but smile Nella, and have a good night."

I am glad Aaron picked it up, since I felt like I was down and out, and didn't like my job.

Mark is being so stubborn; I can't understand it. Mark doesn't appear to have a heart, especially after I wouldn't celebrate. He wants me to feel this is a lowdown, dirty job. So far, this is my hardest night here. I have to wash, dry, and hang the uniforms, but the hardest part is the relationship between me, and Mark. It's different now. He said that I'm part of the team, but he is not being a good teammate. I wonder if he knows he's hurting me, and if he remembers the love we shared. On the other hand, maybe he feels the same way. Finally, I'm done and it's time to go home. Thank God

I am off tomorrow. I'm glad I live close to the ballpark and chose to walk, because it is a beautiful night.

CHAPTER VII

Pick It Up!

On this day off, I will rest and look for a job in the newspaper. I need to pick up something else for the off-season, but I don't see any good jobs. In the future I wish to open a store. With my own designs, however I do feel successful designing the shirt for Mark. As, I lay here thinking about Mark he doesn't want the money back, so I don't want any commission for the shirt, and will continue saving so I can pay him back. "So I write in my journal.

Dear Journal,

Off again today. "Last night, Aaron left something in the dirty locker room and basically saw me at my lowest point, because Mark left his uniform on the floor again." Mark, all I can think about is him; and his uniform on the locker room floor, but that's in the past, Aaron picked it up, and the two of us shared laughter in the short time he was there. Aside from the workload, it was a beautiful night.

THE END

I fall asleep and dream I'm running, and Mark is calling my name: "Nella, Nella!" Then I awaken. What a dream! I slept all day and all night. Strange--in my dream I also thought I was at work and Mark was calling my name. Today, I finally feel rested, and it is time to take a hot bath, wash my hair, and maybe wear some lipstick to feel better. Thank God it's an evening game and I'm here well rested. There's Mr. Don.

"Hello Nella, today you are working all day in the store. You're doing a great job, just don't forget to smile have a good day," he said.

Time is going fast today, and they picked up another win! The store is not as busy and people are smiling also making purchases. I'm happy I don't have to get the dirty uniforms. Besides, I need a break from picking Mark's uniform up from the floor. Poor, Troy maybe will have to pick it up. I'll ask him before he goes home?

"Not again, Mark! Pick it up!"

"What, Aaron?"

"Your uniform, Mark, pick it up!"

"What are you going to do if I don't pick it up, Aaron?"

"I'm going to tell the manager Mark, just pick it up! That's the reason Nella is not working in here." Aaron said.

"Mark, you're always claiming to be better than me, if you are then, pick up your uniform, and throw it in the correct place. The giant hamper!"

"You guys want to know about Nella," Mark said.

A couple of teammates utter, "Yes, Mark--did you get to home base?"

"What can you say about Nella?" another teammate asked. "She's a drama queen! I gave her money!" Mark said.

At this time. STRIKE! Aaron approached Mark, and delivered a resounding blow to his face. Mark has fallen back onto the lockers. "Stop, Aaron! Mark, be quiet, Troy is in the hall, said Josh." Mark picked himself up and uttered," Caught me off-guard Aaron." So what? That's fine. I'm better than you are," said Mark. "Besides, let Troy pick it up! I'm leaving."

With Troy waiting in the hall, Mark angrily leaves the locker room.

"I'll pick it up again!" Aaron said. "I can't believe what he said about Nella. Josh, let me tell you, Mark is always trying to buy someone, like at the bar--drinks for all the girls. I paid for them, and he feels I'm cheap. He is not better than me--I am the better player, and you can bet he'll see he's not."

When Troy came back to the laundry room, I asked. How his day was going? "Great, thanks for asking Nella my day is going well," he replied. "Except in the locker room."

"Nella, I need to tell you something. Today standing in the corridor, I overheard the men talking about you."

"Well, Troy, I've heard that before."

Troy whispered in my ear, "Mark said, he gave you money and you were a drama queen, but Aaron punched him. Mark pushed the door open and stormed out. He saw me in the hall, and gave me that look. He knows I heard them.

Watch out for Mark, Nella. He really looked upset. Girl, I don't know how you do it, this job is exhausting. Nella, here comes Aaron--time for me to go." I thought a drama queen, Mark is wrong. Troy wait a minute. Who picked up Marks?

"Good job today Aaron," Troy said.

"Thanks Troy," he replied. "Nella, I was just checking on you. Where were you?"

"I was working in the store, Aaron."

"Nella, I can't believe I punched Mark."

I pretended that I didn't know. "What?"

"He threw his uniform on the floor again, and I told him to pick it up. He said no! He is very stubborn, but I took care of that."

"I can say I feel good today. We won the game. "Aaron in the same way, I'm having a good day."

"I'm tired of the bar," he said. "How about we go somewhere far away from here for dinner?"

With hesitation, it took me time to answer, but finally I agreed. I thought about how he cared about the way I feel.

"I would love to," I said. I thought how it would be nice to be respected and at least I can have dinner with Aaron, since he told Mark to pick up his uniform. Maybe he won't do it the next time. I arrived back at my apartment to prepare to meet Aaron at the restaurant. I'll wear a dress and my hair up to feel a little formal. With the exception of Mark calling me a drama queen he's wrong, and I don't care to think about it. I'm feeling good and want to stay in this mood when I meet Aaron, mostly because I miss the men.

I met Aaron at a restaurant in the North End. It feels good to be close to my old neighborhood. I am starting to sense my old self returning.

"Seating for one?" asked the waitress.

"No, someone else will be joining me," I replied.

I hope Aaron finds the place.

"There he is," I told the waitress, "Just in time."

I thought about how Aaron is a nice-looking man with a flawless face and a great smile--he seems to care.

"Hi Aaron, find the place all-right."

"What would you like to drink?" He asked.

"My answer was a glass of red wine."

"I'm having a non-alcoholic beer, he said."

"You look nice, Nella."

"Thank you."

"You're welcome."

We started to talk. Aaron told me how happy he is to be moving on to another team and what he dreams of doing when he leaves. He said the first thing he will do is travel when he has another job. I told him how much I liked to design fashion and about my dream of owning a store filled with my designs. I ordered a shot of liquor.

"Would you like a shot of liquor, Aaron?"

"Usually I don't drink the day before the game, but I guess one shot won't hurt."

I'm so comfortable talking to him. We sit and drink shot after shot. Then we ordered a dinner of grilled salmon and fresh broccoli.

"Nella, can I ask you a question? What's going on with you and Mark?"

I knew at some point he would ask that question.

"What did he do for you give you money?"

"No he surprised me with a gift of money," I replied.

"I've known him for a while, and I think he really likes you and wants to get his way. He's a time bomb when he doesn't."

"Aaron, I don't want to talk about Mark. Anyway, I think I had a little too much to drink. When I lived out here, I would walk home; I guess old habits are hard to break."

"I'll take you home."

"Sure, I'll leave my car and key, in front of my old apartment."

"Nella, we're finally here."

"Thanks Aaron. Want to come in for some coffee? I know you have a long drive home."

"Yes, I would love some coffee."

"Well, this is my place--make yourself at home; I'll be right back."

Dizzy, I went to the bathroom, took my clothes off, put on my gown, and jumped in bed. "Nella, is it okay if I lay on your couch to rest for a minute," said Aaron?

"Nella, can you hear me? Nella are you alright? She's asleep Aaron thought, I guess I'll leave her alone anyway it was a long day. The both of us had to work, then the problem with Mark, in the locker room before the game. Drama I can't believe he would make that comment about Nella. I'm glad she didn't hear him, and isn't any of my business to tell her. I will lay here on the sofa for a minute, this feels so right, we won, and I enjoyed the night. Aaron has fallen to sleep.

I can't believe I had fell asleep and awoke the next morning to find Aaron on the couch, sleeping. I forgot about the coffee last night. I went to make him breakfast. I made the best omelet with hash browns and then fresh-squeezed orange juice, and of course, coffee.

"Good morning, Nella, I asked you last night if it was okay to lie on your couch. Sorry I fell to sleep. I looked in, and you were instantly asleep."

"No problem Aaron."

"Can I use your lavatory?"

"Sure Aaron, no problem." How do you like your coffee?"

"I like my coffee black. Here's your coffee. Would you like to eat breakfast? Please eat Aaron--thanks for dinner last night and for staying."

"Nella, this is good. Can you cook? You should cook for the team."

Suddenly, with a burst of tears I cried, "If I'm there next year, maybe I will cook for them."

"Great," Aaron demanded. "Why don't you relax, Nella? Don't cry. I'll be going now so I can rest before the game. I'll see you at work. Thanks for breakfast."

Aaron slept here last night. I hope he has a safe trip home, because I'm feeling like he kept me safe. Aaron asked me, "how I felt about Mark?" He has taken my mind off him--last night Mark didn't exist. I'm hoping the shirt I made for Mark didn't lead him on. Then he wanted something back. I think Mark should be more professional. He has a career, and I'm working to pay for design school, so I can start my own career. Aaron was here last night for me. I feel he cares more about my heart, than us being together.

CHAPTER VIII

Choose, Then Leave

To start the day, I chose to walk to the ballpark again. I left my car and the key to it in the North End, in front of my old place. The neighbors are welcome to use the car until I return for it. Hopefully, the vehicle will help them out. Last night, I enjoyed spending time with Aaron. Now I'm on my way to work. I'm smiling and excited to see Aaron again.

"Hello Mr. Don," I said.

"Nella, Troy is not here, so I need you to start passing out the uniforms and then the attire, please," Mr. Don said. "Here is the last list for attire, Nella the players shouldn't have any requests. As usual, start with Mark."

I must be professional. Breathe! I wonder what kind of day Mark is having, but I'm excited to see the men.

I am kind of ashamed Mark called me that name, but I'm not nervous. Everything is here and the uniforms look nice. I knock on the door to the locker room.

"Come in," said Mark.

"Here's your uniform, Mark."

Then the men said, "Nella, you're back! Good, great, and miss you!"

"Thank you," Mark said with a smile. But I knew that just yesterday he had called me that name. I see Aaron, and my heart is overcome with gladness.

"Here's your uniform, Aaron. Josh, here you are." Aaron told Josh that I can cook, and then Josh told the team.

"Can you cook for us, Nella?" the team asked me.

Smiling, I looked back at Mark. He looked at me with mere disappointment, but I must ignore him.

"Good luck, men. I'll be leaving now to work in the store."

The store wasn't too busy. Arika and I had time to put away overstock for next year.

"Oh my God, Mark!" I hear people shouting, "Mark! Mark!" Arika said, "Nella, here comes Mark. Is he crazy? It's the beginning of the 2nd inning. He looks really mad."

"Nella, I need to talk to you," he said. He grabbed my arm.

"Let go of me, Mark."

He held me tight and wouldn't let go of my arm. Then he took me to the back room of the souvenir store. Mark was serious, and I felt intimidated.

"Going out with Aaron? He asked."

I remained quiet because of the embarrassment. People were listening. Suddenly, he spoke loudly!

"Going out with Aaron?"

"Stop, Mark! Let me go!"

"You shouldn't be in here!"

"Nella you're a!"

"MARK!"

Mr. Don entered the room, and interrupted, "Mark, I think you should leave; you're causing a big scene!"

"Of course," said Mark, then he turned and walked away. I had never been so humiliated in my whole life.

"What's going on, Nella?" asked Mr. Don. It appears in my eyes now, but he pursued me.

"Nella, you should have told us. There is a level that any player is not allowed to go beyond. Just forget about it Nella."

"I can't believe Mark did this; he'll be dealt with. He just left the game and started making a

scene here instead of doing his job--the nerve of him. We don't tolerate this here. Nella, go home and take the next day off." I left embarrassed, hurt and also

violated by Mark. He keeps

hurting me. First, I am going to find Mark and talk to him. I

expect an apology; I caught up with

him as he walked back to the park. I don't understand him.

"Mark, hold on, I want a word with you! Are you

happy now Mark? Don't you have a

heart?"

"No, Nella."

"What's all this worth, Mark? I never meant to

offend you, Aaron and I are friends I love the men

Mark. Why did you embarrass me?" I started to cry.

"I need to see you, Mark."

"Why, Nella?"

"Why do you suppose, Mark? We need to talk; I'm so

distraught. This war we're having needs to stop. Mark,

please!"

"Whenever, tonight," he said.

Breathe! I'll go get my things--my jacket and my hat. Suddenly, I became quiet and I sit.

"Mark, what do you want?" questioned Aaron when he got back to the clubhouse.

"What's the problem?" Mark asked.

"Are you trying to ruin that poor girl's life?" Aaron replied.

"I don't think it's any of your business Aaron," said Mark. "Stay out of my affairs. I'm leaving. Goodbye."

Meanwhile, I'm sitting quietly with my baseball hat, and think, "What will I do now?" Aaron approached me.

"Nella, I never should have told Josh you could cook," he said.

"No, Aaron it's my fault. Maybe Mark thinks he gave me too much. That money or an opportunity to sell the shirt I designed for him."

"He's selfish, Nella. He left the game. It's not your fault."

"Well, I led him on."

"Nella, I have an idea--we'll give Mark his money back."

I'm falling for Aaron in the same way now. More than friends he was in love with me, and now we are kissing.

"Have to go before they miss me, quiet. See you later, Nella."

I'm going to do it--gather my things and take the keys back to security, and inform them I won't be coming back. Choose, then leave I thought and walk back to my apartment. I left the big beautiful, blue ballpark with heartache; in the background I can hear the game. I turned around and felt very confused walking away from one of the best positions that ever has inspired me, being a worker at the ballpark. I have my hat.

What shall I do with my hat? I'll hold it close to my heart. This hat is a very special memory of this place. I tried so hard at this job. I never should have involved myself with

Mark. When I first started this job, brave was the way to go, but I was weak and never should have taken his money. Deep down, inside I didn't follow the rules. I can think of three reasons why I'm leaving. Number one, fraternization with Mark. Two, he made a scene in front of all the customers and staff. Three, the manager probably knows now, of my lack of patience I really should have waited for the check.

On my way back to my apartment I knew that Mark would probably visit sometime this evening so I packed some things including my baseball hat and the original shirt I made for him. More than likely I will not be in this apartment much longer. Doorbell - there he is the man that ruined my job. I was slow to answer. Knock, knock. Just a minute! I am very tense at the moment finally, I opened the door.

"You're going out with Aaron? Then again he said, "I was a--drama queen!" SMACK! I smacked Mark in the face! His face turned red.

"The drama--queen you always wanted" I said. "Now you're a--drama king Mark!"

"EVEN NOW NELLA," he said. "Nella let's stop playing games." Games never started, besides I will not go back to that job because of you not only now everybody knows about the money. My job is history. What else did you tell them? "Mark just, one question? Why did you disrespect me and ruin my job?" Mark remained silent. "That is what I thought, you don't know why. Well I have something for you, take the envelope. Take it! Take it back it's all there!"

"I don't want it! Nella, I meant that money for you to begin."

"I tell you Mark only to work harder, you helped me get started but didn't let me finish.

It was a mistake I took that money. So I choose to leave and give it back." As I picked my bags up and headed for the door.

"Drama! Aaron is playing games Nella, he just wants to win!" Mark said.

"I have to go, Mark." Tension led me to tears. I pushed the door open and ran. Meanwhile, I can hear Mark calling my name. "NELLA, NELLA! Don't leave your place!" I stopped, thinking Nella go back but I remembered promising to meet Aaron, because our agreement was to give Mark back his money back, and I chose to leave with him. What will I do now? This is silly, next go to the hotel room where Aaron had reserved two rooms and left my key at the desk.

"Finally here, breathe I have to calm down, this room is so nice. I can't believe I left at this point. I am laughing. Doorbell, Aaron, it's Aaron! I'm laughing, I paid him back Aaron!" Aaron is laughing as well. I thought this is against the rules. I'm going away with Aaron, and left my place. I know now it's not funny, I should not have done this. I can't stop thinking about Mark; I'm impatient sitting in this chair, so I arise and pace the room.

"Nella, don't worry. Take a shower. He's confused all the time he wants to win but this time he doesn't." Aaron assured me.

"Aaron it's not a game, nobody wins. I'm leaving everything, including design school. Now I'm at this hotel with you."

"Nella, come here. You can open your own store." Aaron went to hug me but, I pushed him away.

"Is this a game, Aaron?"

"Nella, I'm sure that we could start over, it's never too late to make it to the finish line."

"Aaron promise?" I said.

"Take it easy, Nella."

Therefore, I got into a hot shower. Then I feel anguish and can hear Aaron vaguely say, "Nella I left you everything you'll need. I will call you later, Nella?" He peaked in, and asked if I was going to be fine? I was confused and in pieces, because I was sobbing.

"It's going to be fine," Aaron said. "Wait, do you want me to stay?"

"Yes." Before I knew it the moment was clear. Aaron, took his clothes off, and is joining me. Eventually we are walking to the bed.

"Nella, I will take your mind off everything. We are going to leave, start over, and have everything." This beautiful man is in my arms on this bed. He's making love to me. I feel different, safe now. The tears have dried except the last tear which fell from my right eye and rolled down my face. I know I'm in love with him, because I lay next to him asleep in his arms.

That night, I dreamed that Mark was standing over the bed and he said, "Nella I love you." I awoke in a sweat.

"Nella," Aaron says.

"I thought Mark was here." I said.

"Don't think about him, Nella, I'm here. Nella, you are so sweet. I feel really good forget about us, just don't say his name. He is the one that's confused believe me you are worth better." He arose then said he had to work out, get some rest, and go to his room. "Tomorrow I will be back after the last game get some rest Nella, be comfortable."

Tomorrow is here and it's the last game for Aaron. The team has played and won. Aaron has hit a home-run in the 5th forcing two of his teammates to score. Also he is especially excited because the time he spent with Nella and the team has a victory on his last day. Standing in the corridor before the rest of the team arrives to the locker room.

"Josh, unbelievable Nella and I are staying in a hotel, separate rooms, but that didn't stop us from loving each other. The game is off; she's an emotional wreck. Besides, I love her and we're leaving." Aaron said. "The million! Before, Aaron could finish, Josh said, "Silence!" Here comes

Mark. He walked by the two of them talking on his way to the locker room. They stopped the conversation and continued when they didn't see him.

"Aaron, don't stop now when you're doing so well." Josh said.

"Remember a million dollars Aaron, and definitely it was your call."
Josh turned around and is walking to the locker room.

"Josh, wait a minute." Aaron replied, next thought he doesn't care, he'll win and Josh won't have the money. He will change his mind.

Entering the locker room, the team chanted! "This is your last game. "Going to miss you Aaron!" As Mark stood in the corner he remained quiet, and listened. He thought I wonder if they are playing a game. I heard Josh say a million dollars, and doubt it because Aaron is cheap. Aaron expressed with tears in his eyes, "From the bottom of my heart, I'm going to miss you good men." The team were all agreeing, don't beat us too hard, if we play against you next year."

Finally, every player has left except for Mark. He stays to speak.

Mark said, "Cleaning out your locker Aaron?"

"How much did you give her?" Aaron replied, "Nothing Mark, just my heart and that didn't cost anything."

"Aaron, I asked you nicely to stay out of my business."

"Mark, you put your affairs out there not me. You had to tell about that money! False promises you were never serious, but you are always like that you could never really be loyal, and you have ruined Nella's life, and her job. You broke her. She was never here to pick up after you Mark and just remember that day; I picked up your suit off the floor of the locker room. I didn't want to see her cry anymore. She is broken and I'm going to help her pick up the pieces. One more thing, stay away from us with that drama! It's over with you and her now we're moving on."

"Of course you're loyal and don't play games, hope you live happy ever after, Aaron." Mark, on that note, I have to go."

"Well so long Aaron," said Mark.

Doorbell!

"Aaron is that you?"

"Yes," he uttered, "Nella tell me if Mark tries to contact you! Promise me, Nella? He's being foolish! I'm glad it's over with him, let's move on and leave him here. We will celebrate winning the last game tonight, and leave tomorrow morning."

"So soon baby, I replied. What about my car?"

"We'll replace the car, choose then leave Nella," he said. Finally it's time for me to call my travel agent, and make arrangements to leave.

"Where do you want to go?"

CHAPTER IX

Departure

Hawaii, we will start to make our very own life together. Departing the States there is a long plane ride looking over the South Pacific Ocean, but we are flying first class. Aaron and I hold hands. We are very passionate toward each other.

"Both of us are feeling better," Aaron said. "We'll relax and he's on vacation." When we arrived to Hawaii the first two days both of us slept and swam then stayed up all night on the water. The island is so beautiful the water, sand, and waves. The third day of our stay on the island we admire a view of the full moon over the mountains.

"Look, Nella, I want to show you something on the laptop computer. Here is the home I bought for us. They show every room. A heated indoor pool, a big exercise room, and we can pick our own furniture and cars. We can have whatever we like ordered and delivered. Do you like it, Nella?"

"I love it Aaron," I exclaimed. We ran around the island, swam again, and rolled around in the sand.

The departure from Hawaii was a safe trip back, and finally we are in the home Aaron has purchased for me and him. The furniture has arrived along with a sports car and a truck. The home is large. On the first floor a big kitchen, an indoor pool, four bedrooms, four bathrooms and a huge living room create a beautiful space. The home is a basic high rise with a great view of beautiful trees, sand and the ocean. You can look at the city through the glass windows leading to a terrace. The outside has a concrete walk way that flows to an elevator which goes downstairs to the water.

As time passes we share many good times. We have dinner at a variety of restaurants, shop at exclusive stores, then later traveled to two different countries. First it was Fuji. Fuji is so beautiful. We flew in the plane over the South Pacific Ocean again, and stayed on the Lonely Beach. On the Lonely Beach, we made love, no drama. Then on the island was a shop where Aaron and I shopped for clothes and jewelry. Later we would charter a yacht to view and sail on the South Pacific Ocean. Aaron told me he never thought he would experience the actual sight of a whale.

Departing from Fuji, the second trip across the South Pacific Ocean, our next stop was New Zealand. We took a boat ride to the South island, and saw mountains, wild life which included; exotic birds, parrots and the largest existing bird, the Ostrich. There was lots of sunshine. The perfect time of year is in the winter for us to visit New Zealand.

New Zealand was great especially the vineyards too savor natural flavored wines. Aaron does travel in this country several days out of the month.

Tonight Aaron will arrive back. In the meantime, I'm so excited. I miss him and he knows I'm so very lonely. Ring! My phone, I didn't recognize the telephone number on the caller identification.

"Who is this?" I asked.

"Hello Nella, this is Mark!"

"How did you get my number?"

"Nella, wait, don't hang up! I'm just calling to see how you are doing?"

"Mark, please don't call me, I'm finally over what happened. The job was hard to leave. I left the other men Troy, Arika, and Mr. Don."

"What about me, Nella?"

Quietly I said, "Mark, it was hard I was hurt, but I'm better off now so please find it in yourself to feel happy for me." Surprise! I thought, think fast Aaron is here. I said, "I'll call you back Cenita."

"I'm here Nella," said Aaron. "Who was that on the phone?"

"That was my friend, Cenita, from design school" I replied. She was just keeping in touch with me."

"Look what I brought you," he said.

"What have you done now, Aaron?" He has given me a tan color puppy that looks like a miniature chow. He is so cute! "Thank you, Aaron, I miss you." As, usual I jumped in his arms. "What are you going to name him, Nella?"

"I will name him Bamboo. Aaron how was your trip? I will fix us a drink." While I was fixing us a drink Aaron described the trip.

"Nella, I love my new job! The perfect position to play, and too hear the crowds. The peace I feel on the field like on the Lonely Beach, no drama just a baseball game."

I was thinking about Mark calling me, and how I should change my number, or probably tell Aaron he contacted me.

"Thanks for the drink, Nella, I did something else."

"What?"

"How do you like this?" He opened the box. In the box was a ring with a circle of diamonds.

"Will you marry me?" he asked.

"Yes!" I said, "Thank you, Aaron."

"I love you Nella, and look at the puppy he sleeps." Aaron replied, I as well will shower then sleep." I just can't tell Aaron now, and ruin his good day.

"Goodnight, Aaron."

When we awoke the next morning I said, "Aaron I'm glad you're back. I don't know anyone around here yet, and the spring has arrived."

"Nella, I'm serious about us." Aaron replied. Maybe you can meet the families of the team at the game soon, or we can have a baby. I picked Bamboo up and said, "Bamboo is my baby. I love you guys, and my ring I will never take it off. Aaron, I can't wait to plan our wedding. I'm so happy."

Spring is here and Aaron is back to work, he loves his new job, also he likes his new team. The season has started and Aaron is practicing. At this point, I'm planning our wedding and mailing invitations too many including Troy, Arika, and Mr. Don all travel fees paid for them. We are looking forward to the wedding.

Knock, Knock!

"Come-in, Troy I hope your smart ass brought the right shirt this time!" Mark said.

"Hello to you too, Mark, here is you're uniform and your shirt." said Troy.

"Thanks Troy," with a smirk Mark uttered. Troy said. "Nella sent me an invitation."

"Mark responded, so what I've heard that her, and back-stabbing Aaron are to marry, Josh was boasting about them all day." Mark, when Nella was working here at the ballpark she didn't bother anyone; she just did her job. Mark, not only that, she was one of the best ballpark workers we've ever had."

"Troy I don't care!" Mark exclaimed, "It's not my problem she ran off with tight ass Aaron. He couldn't wait to get her in bed!"

"Well, good luck anyway Mark," replied Troy.

"Arika, Mark is not winning I shouldn't of told him that Nella sent me an invitation."

"Troy, he misses Nella. I can't believe her and Aaron are getting married," Arika said. "Why did you remind him Troy? Mark can be a jerk at times but he really liked Nella."

"Well, he sure has a good way of showing it by calling her a--drama queen, and she just wanted to work here at the ballpark." Troy replied. "I'm sure being with Aaron the sky is the limit; tickets all fees paid for the wedding, and I can't wait for departure."

They lost the game only to score one point in the 3rd inning. Mark thought, I can't believe Troy had the nerves to serve me that information before the game. Upon departure from the ballpark disappointed, Mark got in his car, and decided he would go home to drink his big bottle of whiskey, then drown himself in his sorrow.

Driving his car too fast, the vehicle responded, "OVER THE MAXIUM SPEED LIMIT! PLEASE SLOW DOWN."

"QUIET RIGHT NOW CAR!" Mark said. Finally Mark arrived home with feelings of betrayal from Aaron and Nella. Confused, envious, and most of all angry he drunk some of the big bottle of whiskey. He took another drink, and went to get the key from his safe. Mark walked to his trophy case and unlocked it. Then he took two of the team pictures, with Aaron in them out. He spoke among himself quietly.

"I can't believe that mess it all up for me Aaron. He was always the opponent I'll show you drama!" Then he sat down, balled one picture up, also the other. He threw one in the fireplace, plus the other. Then he said, a little louder, "Aaron and his drama of a woman Nella! Go ahead and get married, everybody just forgot about how I felt. Nella, I tried to help you; the most ungrateful drama queen, I've ever laid eyes on. Then he stated, loudly, friends, part of the team!"

Suddenly, Mark Indulged in another drink stood up and boldly went to his closet. Next; he took the original shirt Nella created out of it. Mark has poured whiskey on the shirt, and threw it into the fireplace, with the pictures. Then he lit up a match! Finally, tossing the fire lit stick into the fireplace, sat and drank more whiskey. He laughed, while watching the pictures and the shirt burn up in flames! After that Mark cried with feelings of guilt; he thought I need to change the past Nella I struck out, and burned the original shirt, I'm the one that's ungrateful. Then he fell asleep.

"Nella, are you ready?"

"Hold on, Aaron."

"I have to go, hurry Nella!" Sunglasses Nella?

"Sorry, I'm done." I replied. Finally on our way to Aaron's first game, feelings of being nervous are imminent because of the crowd. I'll wear sunglasses sitting with the other families, because I feel odd sitting here in the ballpark instead of working at the ballpark. Aaron did look up and wave. THEY WON! Happily, we departed from the game finally arriving home.

"Thanks for coming, Nella," said Aaron. "Want to celebrate, Nella?

"No baby, you go and celebrate. I love you."

"Sure you don't want to come?"

"No, have fun Aaron," I stated as he was departing. Except I thought Mark has been calling my phone and I'm going to erase every message he has left.

Before erasing the messages, I listen to a couple of them. The first message he said, how dare you marry my teammate. The second time he said, I love... I didn't listen to the rest of what he had to say. Right away I erased them from my phone. I must remain happy for there is guilt in my heart. I lay here thinking, next week is the game. Aaron will play against his former team. I refuse to go because the embarrassment from the involvement with Mark. Just about the manager and whole team knows he gave me money then I'm to be married to Aaron.

Instead of sleeping I thought about the ballpark mostly being in the locker room with the players, and actually designing the shirt for Mark, he was impressed. I still remember; the situation is unforgettable. Aaron is finally home from his celebration.

"Aaron, did you have fun baby?" I asked. While Aaron takes off, his cuff links, tie, and shirt. He drops his pants, and approaches the bed. "Yes I had fun listening to the men who are happily married with kids talk about their families; they have a right to be proud." I roll over to look at the clock. Bamboo lies next to me. Aaron gets in the bed desperate to make love, kissing me on my neck.

"Aaron have you been drinking?"

"No, I'm thinking about having a baby," and now he's untying my gown. Bamboo jumps off the bed. "I really want a baby." Eventually, we make love, and finally he states--Yes Baby! After we finished, I arose to depart from the bed then Aaron held my arm, pulled me back to the bed, and gave me a big hug.

"Don't leave yet." Aaron says as he falls to sleep. I lay there and think about how he wants a baby. During the morning Bamboo and I arise about eleven o'clock am. I'll have coffee. Bamboo has his breakfast. There is my phone again, it's Mark, I ignore it. He is calling again, so Bamboo and I hurry out the door to take him for a walk.

"Hello Mark, please stop calling me! If Aaron finds out he won't be happy."

"I don't care about Aaron! Nella, I feel like I ruined your life and it was hard starting this year without you there. I know you loved the job."

"Well, I'm never going back, Mark, you ran me out of town and the job."

"Nella, I need you to hear me say I'm sorry. Nella I'm sorry." Very choked up I stopped, and the tears began to fall.

"I'm sorry too Mark, for a long time I was desperate to tell you because I know you can't please everybody, especially me. I can't talk to you Mark. We are free now. I have Bamboo my puppy."

"I'm happy you have a puppy Nella, I have never told you this, but I'm in love with you, and Nella I didn't tell!"

"Well, It's to late Mark. Forget about me. I have to go, goodbye."

"Nella, wait don't hang up!"

As Bamboo and I walk back, feelings of the first day working at the ballpark is Mark, and the turn his position had taken. Between the doubt, success, and the hard work, I lost confidence and fell to pieces, but I'm fine now, only to hope Mark understands.

"Good morning, Nella. Or should I say good afternoon?" Aaron said.

"Aaron, how did you sleep?"

"I can't believe I slept so late."

"Well, you were exhausted baby you need to sleep." Then we sat, and had coffee. That afternoon I wrote in my journal.

DEAR JOURNAL, Yesterday Aaron and, his team were victorious. They won the game. Aaron celebrated then arrived home that night and we made love. Before that, I listened to the messages Mark left me then erased them. This morning I talked to Mark on the phone. Journal I'm confused I love Aaron but, this is happening so fast. I must not think about the past. I'll stay focused on the future.

THE END

CHAPTER X

On, The Edge

Finally! Next week on the edge Mark is thinking he is not ready to be free, and is better than Aaron also, has a game of his own.

"Welcome, can I help you?" asked the sales clerk.

"Yes, I would like to buy an engagement ring," Mark said.

"Do you have a preference in a ring?" asked the clerk.

"Which is very impressive?"

"The rings here start at $250,000, but this beautiful ring is $1,000,000 dollars sir. What do you think?"

"I love it, and that's the one I want," Mark said.

"How would you like to pay for it?" the clerk asked, startled. Mark put his card on the counter.

"I just need you to fill out this paper for a certificate of ownership, and sign it, the clerk said. Then when you present it to the lucky lady, she is to sign it, and send it or bring it in, but you will have all the rights if she doesn't sign it."

"Where do I sign?" asked Mark.

"Right here," the clerk replied. "In the meantime, I need your identification. Would you like a glass of wine, soda, or coffee?"

"Yes, a glass of wine will suit me."

"I'll be right back, and here is your wine."

"Done with this paper, Ms." Mark said. What about another glass of wine with you?

A toast to the ring! She replied. "Yes after your purchase sir here is your card, and I will put this treasure in a ring box."

"Thank you," said Mark, thinking about Nella and giving her one more chance. The weight of what he was about to do was pressing down upon him; the guilt he felt about her leaving the ballpark; her giving him his money back; calling her that name, and leaving her apartment. *Am I doing the right thing?* Mark wondered about burning the only original shirt Nella made for him as the voices in his head grew cacophonous.

"Here is your receipt sir. Congratulations a toast to the ring," said the clerk, raising her glass. "Thank you, Ms. and you have a good day." Mark said.

"Hello, my man, did you track the area of the holder of that cell phone number?"

"Yes sir, Mark," replied the voice on the other end.

"Give me a location every hour," Mark demanded.

The game is tomorrow and I'm on, the edge.

"Nella, are you going to the game tomorrow?"

"No."

Why not?

"Tonight I want to cook dinner for you, something well the day before game. What would you like?"

"Surprise me Nella, I'm on my way to practice but, before I leave you can't run from my former team someday you'll have to face them forget about that money. Nella I love you and will call you later."

"I love you to Aaron." On my way to shop at the market for dinner, the weather outside is warm and sunny. Excited! I'm singing Hum, hum, hum!

Finally I arrive to the market. I'll buy fresh chicken breast to bake in the oven. Next to produce to gather: tomatoes, lettuce and cucumbers for a salad, Italian dressing then strawberries and grapes for fruit. Now to the bakery for a pound cake and fresh bread then non-alcoholic beer and one bottle of red wine, also dog food. Finished! Now it's time to go home, start my dinner, and feed Bamboo. I'm singing, Hum, hum, hum again as I was loading the food in the car.

"Nella it's Mark!" He exclaimed. Suddenly I felt uneasy. I didn't turn around but I asked, "Mark, are you following me?"

"No just picking up something to eat, and I can't believe you're here, Nella."

"Mark I have to go." So I move very fast to put the things in the car, and he is behind me.

"Glad to see me Nella? I'm excited to see you again!" In the meantime Mark has grabbed my arm.

"What are you doing? Mark, let go of my arm!" I yelled!

"I just want to see your ring," he replied.

"See here it is, now I have to go," I exclaimed. "Mark let me go!" No Nella you, shouldn't of never left your apartment, and you never let me explain, the way I feel. Okay Mark I'm here; just explain and let me go!"

"No, Nella not this time!" Again he has my wrist, and I can't pull back he is so strong. He put my finger in his mouth, and with his teeth took the ring off my finger that Aaron gave me.

"Aaron is so cheap, and so is this ring." Then he put the ring in his pocket.

"Mark what are you doing? Give me my ring back or I'll scream!"

"Nella if you scream your precious Aaron will have a problem. I don't trust Aaron."

"Then why are you doing this?"

"Nella, I refuse to be the only one with a broken heart. Aaron's turn."

"Mark, taking the ring won't make you feel any better. Can you just give it back and leave," I said. "Just let me live happy."

"I promise I'll give it back if you go to my room with me for a while. We never spent much time together; maybe we can talk, or you can tell me why you left with my used to be teammate? I would like closure."

"What are you going to do too me, Mark?" He whispered in my ear, "Nella, I love you, and just want to see if you're sure about marrying Aaron. Remember I ran you out of town.

"I want to marry him, I love him. Mark, I'm happy and won't go!"

"I'm taking the ring then." Mark replied. I'm thinking he promised if I go back with him, he would give me my ring back.

"Please keep your promise Mark." He grabbed my hand. On the edge, I screamed! "No don't touch me!" Therefore, we got into a cab and went to his hotel room, but I left my cellphone behind.

"Josh, man is that Nella?"

"Where?"

"Yes, that is Nella with Mark, and I thought she was marrying Aaron.

I'm going to call him, said Josh. He's not answering. I forgot that they are practicing right now. I'll leave him a message. Aaron hello this is Josh, please give me a call back, when you get this message." Josh thought.

I'll give Aaron a fair warning, also he is losing.

"Mark, since we are here now you promised to give me my ring back." I said. He went to his portable safe, and punched in the code. Then he put my ring in the safe, and took a box out. "Nella, I put all my hard work and everything into this to make it up to you." Mark approached me taking my hand, and put a ring on my finger. The ring is beautiful. I feel a bit amused, and a little uncertain. He has intentionally bought me a ring. "Nella, I want to love you.

"Can you wear the ring and let me spend time with you." Mark cried. "I won't bother you anymore."

"You're silly Mark," I replied.

"Be quiet, Nella." He put his hand on the top of my head then lightly pushed my forehead back, and began to kiss me, just like the first time, because of doubt I hesitated to open my mouth. Mark said "Not this time Nella" so he squeezed my cheeks with his finger and thumb. My mouth opened, and he put his tongue in my mouth to kiss me again. I'm so tired of this; I just stood there, and he undressed me. Then put me on the bed. It happened again. The moment I remember with Mark, physically and emotionally, but my body has belonged to Aaron. I didn't have any energy to resist him.

"Nella, I missed you I knew that day I left the linen room at the ballpark."

"Mark, please I learned Aaron is who I want to be with, this is not a game." He replied. "Aaron is playing games, and he is striking out, he thinks he's better than me. Don't say his name Nella learn me, and forget about him. You were always mine. *You're marked already.*"

"Nobody wins Mark please let me up! What are you doing?"

"Wait Nella relax!" I couldn't move. Then he said, "I'm done." He arose to allow me off the bed. I ran to the bathroom, and was so angry that I knocked everything off the sink. I felt sick. Then I jumped in the shower too try to wash off the past, put my clothes on, and finally took his ring off. I had to regain my composure to get my ring back. I put his ring on the dresser and reminded him I have to go now.

"May I have my ring back?" I asked.

"Pick up the things in the bathroom you knocked off the sink."

"How dare you Mark, so I guess you forgot about the times I picked up after you?"

"Nella you picked my teammate up!"

"Mark just so you know your teammate, Aaron picked me up. That day in the dirty locker room, when you

threw your dirty uniform on the floor for me to pick up;
Aaron picked it up."

"Not again I've already heard that from your
precious Aaron!" Mark yelled. So I took a deep breath, and
gathered the things from off the bathroom floor. He opened
his safe.

"Take it! You'll do it to me and Aaron for a ring."

"Guess you got what you wanted then," I said as I ran
out the hotel and caught a cab back to my car.

"Hello, Josh this is Aaron. Did you call me?"

"Aaron I hate to tell you this, but I saw Nella going in
our hotel with Mark." Aaron was devastated!

"What room?"

"Come on now man you know, I can't tell you that."
Josh said. "Thanks for informing me." On, the edge Aaron
took a deep breath, and raced to the hotel. He has arrived

with sun glasses on alone, with just him and the clerk at the desk.

"Sir I'm a friend of Mark's and forgot his room number," Aaron demanded.

"Aaron is that you? It happens to be you are my favorite player but I'm afraid I can't give out that information however, I can call him."

"No! It's a surprise," Aaron exclaimed.

"Well the game tomorrow is sold out," said the clerk. Aaron replied," but I happen to have two tickets to the game; and two hundred dollars."

"Between you, and me Aaron room number thirty."

"The money and the tickets are right here," said Aaron. The clerk replied, "thank you Aaron much luck to you, hope you get them!"

Aaron proceeded to room 30. Knock! Knock!

"Open the door, Mark!" Aaron yelled.

"What do you want Aaron?"

"Where is Nella? Open the door!"

"Keep your voice down, she took a shower and left, said Mark."

"Open the damn door!"

"Funny, she let me take your ring off her finger then, I put my ring on her finger, and she didn't like my million dollar ring, so I guess yours was better, Aaron."

"What is that supposed to mean, Mark?"

"Figure it out Aaron, and be quiet you might cause a scene." At a lower volume Aaron said, "Mark it happened I and Nella so get over it already."

"Well Aaron you went right behind me, my teammate, great back up."

"Mark you never loved her."

"How do know, Aaron?"

"You trashed her life back at the ballpark."

"Aaron just leave me alone, I have to rest for the game."

"Open the door Mark! Forget it Mark. "Just forget about opening the door Mark, save it for the ball game. "What will you do at the game Aaron?"

"Nothing Mark, I'm done playing games." Aaron I come to think Nella is confused," uttered Mark. Aaron becomes silent. Then he walks away. As he walked a couple of steps, he turned around. Then Aaron goes back to room thirty, taps on Marks door. Tap! Tap! He said. "Mark, one more question? Why would you say she is confused?"

"We made love, she loved it, and she's marked already and will never forget it." So Aaron turned around again, finally walking his way down the hall to leave the hotel. Aaron wonders if Mark knew he pursued her as well, and if he informed Nella. Therefore, Aaron took a deep breath and thought, Nella you were right nobody wins, and I'm sorry baby. I'm tired. So he made his way out to his car thinking he's sort of ashamed of himself, and it's not worth the game.

I must move quickly Aaron will be here shortly, and I never called him back. It's time to cook the food, so I'll put the chicken in the oven, make the salad then I'll spread the fruit and bread on the platter. The beer and wine must go in the freezer now. I'm late because of Mark. Instead of him resting for the game, he wanted to play games with me again just like at the ballpark. I can't think about Mark ever again. How dare him do this to me, but I got my ring back. Finally, I fed Bamboo he was starving. I have to hurry and change clothes something Aaron would like for me to wear. I know exactly what to put on this beautiful color dress, with these white shoes.

As I look in the mirror I take a deep breath, the tears began to fall, I don't look happy or like I've had any rest. I hope Aaron doesn't see it in my eyes that something is wrong because again I feel like I was down and out, so bravery is the best option; most important I can't fall apart. Alarm! I jumped my chicken is finished. Next I'll take the wine and beer out of the freezer. Now I must get my phone to call Aaron.

"Nella!" It's too late to call him he's home.

"How was practice?" I asked as I went to hug him but, he pushed me away. Right at that moment I knew he known something.

"Why didn't you answer my calls?" He said with hostility.

"Sorry, baby I left my phone in the car when I was in the market shopping." I feel of fright so I picked Bamboo up for comfort; Bamboo is shivering. Then I said, "I cooked dinner and here is a beer for you." Aaron took the beer then asked, "Nella where have you been?" I hesitated to answer. He said, "Have you been with Mark?"

"Baby."

"Wrong answer, Nella, I'm not your baby!" he exclaimed.

"Aaron, he's insane I tried to tell you he was calling me, but at the end of the day, it was never a good time. He followed me to the market grabbed my arm, took my hand, and actually my ring off my finger."

"What were you doing in his hotel room?"

"How did you know that?"

"My whole former team knows. They saw you with him!" I thought I've forgot about the team again.

"Just to get my ring back," Mark said.

"If I didn't go with him to his room, he wouldn't give me my ring back. I swear Aaron, I just wanted my ring back understand, because he put it in his pocket."

"What about his ring, Nella? He told me it cost a million dollars."

"That silly ring Aaron?"

"Nella, the silly ring; it couldn't have been that silly. Mark told me he put it on your finger." The distress is near for both of us, eventually I was quiet. "Did you sleep with him?"

"What?"

"It's a yes or no question, Nella? Did you sleep with him?"

"Forget it Aaron, please I have my ring back now."

"I don't care about the ring!" Aaron is really angry. "Answer me!" I flinch then, put Bamboo down. Bamboo runs!

"Aaron you're scaring us!"

"I'll ask you one more time? Did you sleep with Mark? Answer me!"

"Yes! Just like the first time it happened again!"

"No, NELLA. NO!" Aaron exclaimed loudly. With the beer in his hand on the edge, Aaron has taken the bottle of beer, and threw it across the room at the wall! Glass shattered and beer splashed everywhere! I turned to look at him in panic, with my hands over my mouth taking small breaths then begin to sob. With tears in his eyes he said, "Nella, I don't need this stress." Finally he sat, and stated, "OH, NELLA, you should leave."

"Aaron, you told me to leave everything behind. My job, my apartment, my car, design school, and leave with you. Were you serious?" I asked.

"That included Mark."

"Where will I go? Aaron, it's not my fault he followed me to the market, and I don't know how he got my number!" Still I was crying and said, "I left everything for you."

"Just go back to the Northend," stated Aaron.

"What about the wedding?"

"The wedding is off!"

"I sent the invitations out already."

"I'm sure everyone will hear the news."

"What about Bamboo?"

"Take him or leave him, Nella." I move to hug Aaron. He said, with a cold heart, "No you let him touch you."

"Is this a game, Aaron? Now I have to start over again?"

"Nobody wins, Nella!"

"I want us to win, get to the finish line."

"Nella, you are not finished with Mark, just take this card."

"NO, YOU'RE JUST LIKE HIM!" I cried out! "You both took advantage of me!" Then I took a breath, and said, "Aaron, don't let this break us apart, like an arrow in my heart is it worth it. I don't want your money! I just want to go back to the first day I started at the ballpark! I miss the laughter, love, and the team winning, so I wonder if things could have been different."

"Nella, I'm tired and confused, and sorry. Please don't be here when I get back. I have a game tomorrow and can't rest with you here."

"Fine! I'll go Aaron, but I feel like you and Mark took advantage of me." He remained quiet then put the card on the table and left. Mostly important now, I must gain my composure and at the same time breathe. I thought to myself, Nella you must be brave while this storm is going on inside of you. First, I will pick up this mess and put the food away. Second, I will pack my things, especially the original shirt I designed for Mark; this design is an example of my work for the future. Third, I'll get the money card Aaron left. Finally, I'll make reservations for a flight back to the Northend. So I, and my most noble now; and useful Bamboo can leave. I put on my sunglasses, and left the keys. Then I picked Bamboo up. I took a cab to the airport, as we went through to transfer Bamboo was clinging to me. Then he had to be put in the cage in order for him to travel home safe. Most of all times during this journey I've felt unsteady, unwise, and most of all upset. I boarded the flight, sat down and, wept. I'll take my journal out and write in it.

Dear Journal,

It is midnight. I was fortunate to book a late night flight home to the Northend for me and Bamboo, so time for me to move on again. Three things I know belong to me, my baseball hat a reminder of being a ballpark worker. I remember the first day starting having feelings of doubt about the job. The short time at the ballpark I did enjoy working there. The original shirt I designed for Mark made me feel successful, and sold out on the first day. I have my puppy Aaron gave me for company, but he preferred it was time to have a baby. I made a mistake being with Mark again this afternoon, now the love Aaron shared with me these past months is no more.

THE END

The paper is soaked with tears. I stopped writing. Then I said to myself, be brave Nella, accept responsibility for your actions; no more sobbing or drama. On the edge, I refuse to take the identity of a woman scorn with these sunglasses on wishing nobody, on the plane can see me cry. The flight attendant did bring me a single box of tissue but, before that my journal was wet from my tears. The plane carried me, and Bamboo back to the Northend. I left my journal on the plane. So I took the rest of the money that Aaron gave me to start over and temporarily stayed in a hotel. Later I got another apartment, opened an original design store and partnered with Cenita. So bitter sweet in the meantime I am happy but still feel the pain of heartache. I found out I'm having a baby and I am grateful to have Cenita to help me. Except she keeps asking "Nella, when are you going to tell Aaron you're pregnant?"

"I don't know, Cenita." I say with tears in my eyes. To the point I think about Aaron, and sometimes Mark. But in the same way they have not tried to contact me. I have not tried to contact them.

"THE END"

Here is a sneak peek from, *Nella: A Ballpark Worker Book I, Five Drama Fiction Short Stories Segments Uncut Version*:

I, the Flight Attendant, and my coworkers perform the usual walk to check for belongings left behind on the plane after passengers EXIT. There was a book she left. Barely could I see the writing. It belonged to the young lady wearing sunglasses. I thought, *what could have been wrong with her? Maybe she has a fear of flying in a plane or relationship problems.*

"Be at ease Ms. Is there something wrong?" I asked.

"My puppy is flying separate." she responded. At the time I remember thinking her animal will be fine. I picked the book up opened it and looked for a name or address. IT READS AS FOLLOWS...

Coming Soon From Knack-Time Books:

Nella A Ballpark Worker Book I, Five Short Story Segments Uncut Versions

LASTVIEW (Drama Fiction)

SHARKEY STREET; WHERE I'M FROM, A TRUE STORY. (Geography Non-Fiction)

Nella A Novella Day Book II, (Drama Fiction)

I invite you my readers to express comments at:

Twitter: @KnackTime (contest and more)

Facebook: Candace Taylor Johnson

Thank you KnackTime Books

About the Author

"My name is Candace Taylor Johnson, and I was born in Anderson, Indiana. At the age of six I traveled with my family to Clinton Township, Michigan. I enjoy living in Michigan, known as THE GREAT LAKES. I like residing near Lake St. Clair where we enjoy fishing on the lakes. Special harvest includes walleye, salmon, catfish, and pickerel. Lake St. Clair is also known for, swimming and boating. The Lake flows on the Blue Water, where we reach the Blue Water Bridge leading over to the Province of Ontario. Similar to other states, Michigan is filled with the most unique people of different cultures, and we all revolve inside and outside of Detroit. I have many interests which include music, sports, cinema, and the art of literature also the presence of Gods nature. I am a proud mother of five boys my cherished treasures, as well as my brothers and sisters. In the future I look forward to composing Novellas "New" fiction, and non-fiction, literature that will interest the reader. Books rich enough for you to experience, and have as a keepsake."

"Sincere Thank You, Candace Taylor Johnson"

Available: www.CreateSpace.com/3787902
Amazon.com
Look for in participating Book Stores, all over the world.
"I also want to send a special thanks to everyone that has chose to read this Novel, Nella A Ballpark Worker Book I."
A Sneak Peek
"Nella A Novella Day Book II."
"Whiskey shots keep them coming,"stated Mark.
"Mark I haven't seen you in a while."
"Well these days I don't feel much like celebrating keep them coming," he uttered.
"Here you go."
"Thanks," said Mark.
"No problem." The bartender said. "Can I ask you a question?
What ever happen at the game Aaron and Josh were playing?
Which game? Mark asked?   ,
"The million dollar game." The bartender said.
"Something about a girl named Nella."
The bartender explained.
"Well between me and you it went like this…"Gladly Mark thought. Time to find one of the best designers to design an outfit for that baby!